Per aspera ad astra

Cicerone, Seneca

1

Lorenzo Bortolotto

Caressing the Clouds

A story

In memory of two fallen friends

Alice is at the airport waiting to welcome her sister back from the USA. As she walks from the parking lot to the terminal her eyes move towards the sky and focus on the clouds.

She would like to see the airplane landing, but she remembers when she was a child laying down on the grass and starts to daydream, getting lost among the clouds.

Her paper airplanes, her kite and the dandelion showerheads that as a child she enjoyed spreading on the lawn, have not been flying for a long time.

In the sky above her house, instead, strange contraptions called hang-gliders and paragliders are flying freely.

While yesterday she only imagined herself caressing the clouds, today those daredevils can really touch them with their hands.

Her thoughts run backwards.

And they remind her that someone in the past did enable her to touch the clouds. Not from the ground, standing on the grass, but really flying high in the blue sky.

Alice flying! She who had always been afraid of voids.

There is a mountain overlooking the Venetian plain and if you climb, even without going too high, you can see the Venice lagoon towards the east, or the Berici mountains to the west and the Euganean hills to the south.

On the horizon, when there is good visibility, you can even see the outlines of the tallest buildings in Padua.

The top of that massif is Cima Grappa.

And there, in the quiet, there stands a majestic ossuary where the remains of innumerable soldiers who died during the Great War rest.

On the two sides of this mountain two rivers flow, the Piave and the Brenta. Which were also made famous by the war.

Over the Brenta there is a famous wooden bridge which was built a long time ago to join the two halves of a city called Bassano del Grappa.

That small community still have their beautiful wooden bridge: periodically it needs maintenance, owing to the raging seasonal floods that the locals call *brentane*.

The pretty city is a destination for crowds of tourists, who visit it for its historical and gastronomic peculiarities.

Among its most characteristic and appreciated products, which visitors taste and then take home, are Marostica cherries, white asparagus and *grappa*, a sour-flavored brandy.

In addition to traditional historical-gastronomic tourism, a completely different variety of tourism has made its appearance over the last few decades.

In the early eighties of the last century, some daring young people began to gather at the foot of the imposing massif, from whose slopes they launched themselves and took flight aboard their hang-gliders.

Hang-gliders are basically large triangle-shaped kites, with a lightweight aluminum frame covered with a synthetic fiber sheet.

The latter is mounted directly on the spot. After that, pilots attach themselves to the machines and launch themselves along a slope, to then take off and fly.

Some time later the paraglider was invented, a kind of parachute made in the shape of an orange wedge which made the flight cheaper and faster to set up, as the glider can be enclosed in a backpack so is easy and comparatively light to carry.

Since that time these skies have become increasingly crowded with strange flying humans who sometimes run the risk of colliding with each other in the air.

Or falling to the ground.

When the ambulance arrived at the scene, its sirens just silenced, the young man who had fallen with his paraglider had already regained consciousness.

Some people had gathered close to him, maybe friends, maybe just onlookers.

The rescuers immediately asked him if he remembered his name and if he felt any pain.

Then they took off his helmet and carefully began to detach him from the paraglider harness.

Finally they put a brace around his neck and strapped him to the stretcher.

The young man asked to be transported to the Bassano del Grappa hospital, for reasons of his own that he could not explain at that dramatic moment.

The ambulance, which came from the first aid post closest to the paragliding and hang-gliding area, headed for the Bassano hospital with its sirens on.

The reason why the paraglider wanted to be carried to that hospital did not seem to be of much interest to the rescuers: perhaps they indulged him because he was at risk of death, or maybe that hospital was indeed more largely and better equipped than other closer ones, so the doctors there could face the emergency with a greater chance of success.

During the ride with sirens blaring the paraglider pilot lost consciousness again and went into cardiac arrest.

The ambulance rescuers did everything to save the young man's life and when they arrived at the hospital everything was ready to try to revive him.

Not very far from that place, many years back, a little girl is running happily in the backyard.

And there a spiteful gust of wind entangles her magnificent kite, given to her by her father, among the branches of a tall tree in the garden.

The girl tries to pull the thread to free it, but realizes that she could break it.

In the end she decides to call her dad who, ever ready to remedy the problems in the family, arrives on the scene smiling.

"Don't worry, now I'll get a ladder and we'll take it down."

And so the kind man goes away, only to return shortly after with the long tool.

Climbing the ladder, he approaches the thick canopy of the tree and reaches inside to get at the nylon thread annoyingly entangled around a branch.

It won't take him long to free the wonderful toy that he himself has built for his daughter: just unravel the tangle of thread and the kite will fall to the ground, so it can be retrieved by the child.

It all seems so easy.

The tragic news came from her sister, who had lived in the United States for many years: her nephew had died in a plane crash.

Her only nephew, her sister's only child, whom she had only seen in photographs as a child and never in real life, had died on his way to picking up a scholarship in Chicago.

The young man had moved to the Great Lakes region precisely for study purposes.

He had flown from San Francisco, where he had spent a few days with his mother, and was returning to Chicago where he was to receive an award for his research on butterflies.

It had been a tragic accident, in which over a hundred people had lost their lives.

Her nephew was a young and promising entomologist who studied the monarch butterfly, a type of moth that every year, to overwinter, makes one of the most extraordinary migrations in the world: thousands of kilometers traveled by a single generation of butterflies, from the region of the Great Lakes in North America to Mexico.

For a moment her thoughts shifted from the tragedy that touched her so closely.

She had the vision of a billion butterflies flying from those places in the north of the American continent and pushing towards a single mountain in Mexico to spend the winter.

She knew that on that occasion the trees of the mountain were literally invaded by swarms of butterflies.

Her nephew's idea was based on following the three successive generations of monarch butterflies, those who return from Mexico to the Great Lakes region, using drones.

It was a research project he had devised himself and which was called **Angel**.

The boy had been attracted to butterflies from a very young age: many times, as a child, he had risked stumbling or bumping into obstacles to chase them.

And when he was still a child he had begun to ask his mother questions.

He wanted to know where his father was, and she replied that he had flown away just like butterflies do.

That he had flown like an angel to heaven.

Then, when he brought home the butterflies he had caught, he told her that they were angels, and his mother hugged him tenderly and whispered: "You .... are my angel!".

Perhaps it was for this reason that the young researcher had given that name to his project.

The sky, as we know, has always fascinated mankind in the most varied forms of imagination: it was believed that only deities and angels could live up there.

Today, however, even that formerly forbidden place can be inhabited by human beings.

Yet, at times, with tragic results. One example are the flying accidents involving paragliders that have occurred repeatedly in recent years.

Especially from the beginning of spring and then for the whole duration of the summer. Those seasons see a steady increase in the number of flights and consequently in the number of pilots falling from the sky.

In winter these accidents are not nearly as frequent, precisely because there are fewer people flying. Certainly the cold and bad weather discourages these activities, just as many outdoor sports slow down quite a bit in the coldest months.

Only the most daring and those with the longest flying experience, who also participate in international competitions, continue to attend even the cold winter skies to train.

Just at the foot of that now well-known mountain, there is a small town.

It is near Bassano, on the border between

the provinces of Vicenza and Treviso, and is very popular with paragliders and hang gliders from all over Europe.

Around that place there are several suitable spots from which to launch and many fields on which to land, and there are also competitions involving duration of flight and distance from the launching spots.

Of course, to be able to practice this sport you must first attend specific courses and obtain a pilot's license, as well as equip yourself with an emergency parachute.

There are some flying schools where one can learn to practice this discipline.

When latter-day Icaruses are engaged in competitions in the spring, the sky above the mountain turns into an anthill so teeming with life that it is almost impossible to count them.

It truly is a sight to see.

Among the many dazed onlookers with their noses up, that day there was also a young local woman: her home was located right in that village at the foot of the famous mountain.

She had always liked looking at the sky, especially as a young girl, when she lay on the grass looking at the clouds and fantasizing. With her imagination she could see anything in the changing shapes of the clouds, and she just had to stretch her hands upwards to touch them.

In her childhood fancies she dreamed one day of making a kite so big that it would touch the clouds and caress them.

Just like those people up there were doing.

Try to imagine blowing on a dandelion flower, the kind that are collected by children in the fields in spring. The seeds fly off the white sphere, just like those little individuals hanging from their fluttering colored parachutes.

And while her gaze was blissfully lost, the woman who lived in the village remembered a few lines by a young local author, who had written a poem in the Venetian dialect, devising a simile between a flower head scattering its seeds in the wind and a father abandoned by his children.

How did the poem go? Ah yes....

There is a flower

planted in the corner of a house

that has around its crown

so many seeds to fill a field,

collected in a lifetime.

But all of a sudden

a gust of wind detaches them from their father

to take them to a foreign field.

The old stem

stripped of its possessions,

in two or three days

will be as dead

as a dead dog.

But it's not sad

because it knows

that they have not been thrown away:

they'll make a family

in a distant place.

She liked the poem a lot but it also made her a little sad because it reminded her of her dad who was gone.

But then she shook herself and resumed watching the paragliders floating a few meters above the ground right above her garden, to land on the strip of field near her house.

She was fascinated to see them fly, but only from her point of view, that is from below.

The young woman's name was Alice, she worked at the Bassano del Grappa hospital, and whenever an accident happened to one of those daredevils near her home and she heard the ambulance siren or the sound of a rescue helicopter, she felt a shiver.

Her heart squeezed as if in a vice as she heard the mournful howl of the siren.

She spent a good part of her Sundays observing, through binoculars, the colorful paragliders circling in the sky. She was enraptured by the sight.

They were beautiful to look at... However, she preferred keeping her feet firmly on the ground.

She knew that some were losing their lives and that many suffered serious and permanent injuries.

She saw them when they arrived at the hospital where she worked as a nurse in the emergency room. She did not understand why people risked what is most precious to them, life.

For the sheer thrill of it, probably.

Or maybe because they wanted to feel stronger or braver than others?

She knew she too was courageous, in her heart, despite her somewhat shy temperament: she had never had great passions or great loves, only a few small youthful stories.

She preferred to live her life between staying at home, busy with her chores, and working in the hospital.

Alice had just turned thirty. She was a pretty girl, but - as mentioned - she was not an experienced woman.

In spite of the few flirtations, she was by no means aloof or sullen: she was simply the kind of woman who goes out of her way to go unnoticed.

In short, she did not show off, unlike so many of her peers.

It was necessary to look deeply into her eyes and see her smile to understand where her beauty was hidden.

20

Her physique was lean, her brown hair matched her hazel eyes, and her temper was gentle but firm.

A solid type, in a word, and in her own way a fascinating one.

One day, in the hospital, Alice met a young man who had fallen with a paraglider. Luckily, he had managed to trigger the reserve parachute and fallen onto a tree.
The guy had gotten away with some broken ribs.

During the few days of his stay in the hospital, Alice visited him in the ward.

Maybe she did so because the young man seemed nice, or because he had nice clear eyes, or maybe because she was driven by curiosity and wanted to know what drove him to risk his life.

The nurse greeted him and then looked at him cheerfully.

"Hi, I'm Alice and I work in the ER. How are you doing? You were lucky and I think you must have gotten a good scare!"

The young age of the man had already helped him resume his boldness, so much so that he allowed himself to joke with the unknown nurse.

"And my name is Angelo", he replied. "I confess that I had already taken into account that sooner or later it could happen, but this time I didn't want to pull out my wings, otherwise everyone would have realized that I am really an angel. It was enough for me to operate the emergency parachute!"

He gave her a cheery smile.

"Ah, I understand. However, I don't think it's enough to be called Angelo to avoid dangers, otherwise all parents would call their children that, wouldn't they?", she retorted. And then, after a smile accompanied by an amused grimace, she went on: "Maybe you want to show someone or yourself that you have guts."

"Maybe. But it certainly doesn't take a lot of guts to cut and sew other people's skin", replied the young man insolently. "I risk my skin to have fun, it's true, but without hurting anyone else."

Alice wanted to retort by slamming in his face her opinion against practicing such risky fun, but she gave it up.

She thought that after all he was indeed risking his own life: she had recognized in his eyes the typical swagger of young people.

Angelo had to be careful how he breathed, because even just laughing caused him acute pain due to his cracked ribs. Sure enough, every now and then he asked to be given painkillers.

Sometimes Alice, knowing about this problem, maliciously tried to make him laugh to see him suffer. But hers was not evil for its own sake: she only hoped to make the young man reflect.

In the end Angelo no longer asked for injections against the pain in his chest which, a bit perversely, she herself was causing him. It almost seemed as if she enjoyed looking for him in the wards to see the terror of the syringe in his eyes.

Despite these skirmishes between the two, a sort of mutual sympathy was born, even if they understood that they had two opposite views on how to live life: she preferred to have a bottom-up, down-to-earth point of view, whereas he aspired to have a point of view from above, to look down on the smallness of people and the insignificance of their anxieties.

On his last day in hospital, when Angelo went to say goodbye to Alice, he invited her to visit him at the airfield where the paragliders were hovering in the air.
She thanked him and said she would think about it.

Alice soon forgot that acquaintance she had made in a hospital setting.

One Sunday morning after mass, inspired by the beautiful spring day and driven by curiosity, she decided to get into her car to just go and take a look at the place up in the mountain from where those daredevils launched themselves. What moved her, she thought, was a desire to understand the motives that led them to take so many risks.

On the first runway, as she drove up the road from below, there were many paragliders getting ready. She looked at these young people from many countries, speaking several European languages and all of them smiling and joking. No one seemed to be afraid or even worried about jumping into the void.

Alice parked her car park along the hang-glider runway, which was higher than the paragliding runway and occupied by fewer vehicles. This was due to the fact that the paraglider, a latecomer, had become more and more popular because it was less expensive to buy and a lot easier to transport and mount.

Seeing a hang-glider pilot engaged in preparations for the launch and saying hello to a friend in Italian, the girl approached.

Driven by curiosity, she asked him kindly: "Excuse me, are you throwing yourself off now?"

The young man, with a sustained and pedantic air, seeming almost offended, replied: "We don't throw ourselves, we take off!"

So she waited for the guy to take off and then moved to the paragliding runway, hoping to find someone less touchy and more talkative. There she came across many young people who were busy preparing for their turn to launch, laughing and joking. It felt like a wholly different atmosphere, so Alice sat down on the grass and watched them.

It was natural for her to smile, because some of them were doing a bit of a show – in an almost clownish way, it seemed to her, even if she didn't understand what they were saying. She was not the only one sitting on the grass of the slope watching, there were numerous other young people who, like her, enjoyed the spontaneity of the proceedings.

She had been there for a while when a pilot with a bigger paraglider than the others came to settle down on the runway. A girl approached him shortly thereafter.

In a few minutes they were both tied to the big harness, with the girl in front of the pilot and behind them the paraglider stretching out on the grass.

Alice heard them speaking Italian, and when they were ready to take off, the girl who was in front of the pilot turned to greet her friends with a ringing "ciaooo". A boy sitting on the grass next to her answered the greeting and sent back to her an equally resounding "ciaooo".

Then the pilot and the girl looked at the wind vane flag on the sidelines. As soon as a gust of favorable wind arose, the pilot urged the girl in front of him to run down the mountainside together, and at the same time raised his arms, which were holding the control lines of the paraglider.

After a few meters the bright red paraglider swelled up suddenly and immediately after the two people's feet were lifted from the ground and began to fly towards the sky. Alice, too, felt her heart lighter as she imagined the sensations the girl had just felt, and smiled.

Turning her head she saw that a boy sitting on the grass not far away was smiling too, but to her. She looked at him carefully: brown hair, clear eyes, athletic body and .... spontaneous ways. Sure enough, he rose nimbly and came towards her.

"Hi, do you remember me? I'm Angelo."

Then the young man sat down next to her, continuing to talk to her, smiling and holding out his hand.

"We met in the hospital! I'm the one who had some broken ribs .... now I'm fine again and those two people you saw take off earlier are my friends, the craziest I could find!"

"Hi Angelo .... of course I remember you, how are you?", She answered shaking his hand.

"Would you like to be in that girl's place? Would you like to fly like her? But maybe it takes too much guts, huh?, asked the young man with a mischievous grin.

Alice noticed that he had a peculiar way of smiling, unsymmetrical and very sly, as it were.

"I would love to, but I'm too scared!" she replied sincerely.

"I used to be a bit scared too, but after taking a run you will realize that fear will give way to wonder."

"Yes, but..."

"You won't be afraid to go for a run, I hope! It's just about running! Like when you ran after me with the syringe in your hand!", Angelo continued bursting into laughter.

This time she joined the witty young man in
28

laughter.

"I would love to try, I'm serious, but another time. Now I have the car here and then I would have to come back to pick it up. Maybe next time I'll ask a friend to give me a lift, so I can show you that I have some guts too".

What Alice was actually doing was find excuses to avoid flying.

"Then I'll leave you a note with my friends' phone numbers and mine. We do test launches for those who want to have a fantastic but safe first experience in flight ... you'll see that you'll like it."

The woman said goodbye to the young man, who pronounced his *arrivederci* with the rounded r's typical of German and French people. But as she watched him turn and go it did not occur to her to ask him where he was from. Would she ever find out?

Just a week later Alice was back on that hill where the daredevils were paragliding, hoping to meet the attractive young man who had inspired her a lot of sympathy and to try her first flight. This time, however, she had brought her friend Marta with her.

When she did find Angelo she asked her friend to take the car back to the airstrip near her house once she had taken off. She felt a little nervous and in her heart she wondered what had placed her in that situation. Was she really testing her courage or had she been lured there by Angelo's eyes and peculiar smile?

She was excited and a little trembling as she listened to the instructions the young man was imparting on her. When he gave her the go she started running at full speed and screaming at the top of her voice down the slope, until her feet no longer touched the ground. She found herself tripping for a few more steps into the void.

When she felt the pull of the sail she understood that they were getting up and looked first at the sky then at the ground. She turned to look at Angelo's face and saw that he was smiling at her.

Her heart, which had previously been

galloping, slowly began to feel lighter and
calmer as the trees and people grew smaller
and smaller.

The atmospheric visibility was perfect that
day. Angelo pointed to the lagoon.

"Can you see Venice?"

She nodded as the paraglider turned north.
Then he asked her if she recognized the snow-
capped mountains in the distance,

"I know Mount Grappa only!", she replied.
"By the way, where are you from? You look
German!"

He smiled broadly and explained: "Many
take me for German, but in fact I'm from
Venice. My mother, it is true, is German ... she
fell in love with an Italian-American, that's
why I look a bit ... Nordic. "

Alice looked at him amusedly and asked him
to tell her more.

"The house where I was born is in Bolzano,
but I have been living in the lagoon for many
years now. Where are *you* from?"

"Can you see that house down there? With
that front lawn and that vegetable garden?"
She said, pointing with her hand to a small
house far below them. "That's where I live
with my family."

31

"Would you like us to land just in the garden of your house?" he asked.

"No, we'd better not, they don't know I'm flying. Besides, my friend will be waiting for me on the airstrip."

When they landed Marta was there waiting for them with a big smile, which Alice returned. She was happy and wished the flight had lasted longer.

Angelo told her that he was already looking forward to an encore: next time, however, she should stay longer, because among his friends it was customary to celebrate the baptism of flight of those who, like her, had just started. The date of the party would be arranged together with the others.

"It is a ceremony which aims to be propitiatory for the good fortune of future paragliding pilots!" sentenced Angelo proudly.

She said goodbye to him promising that she would be back soon for more flights, and then ran to join Marta. The two friends embraced and Alice began to jump, trying to get her friend to join her in the dance and share her joy.

"It was wonderful, Marta! You must try it too!", shouted the new flyer.

Marta smiled, but she was a little

bewildered as she witnessed Alice's metamorphosis from caterpillar to butterfly. It was obvious that the flight had done her good, she thought, because she had never seen her so euphoric. She had known Alice as the epitome of calmness.

Chapter 12- HOPES AND UNCERTAINTIES

Within a few days Alice's euphoria and pride in her courage subsided and the second-thought stage took over. She realized that flying was a risky activity, as she had learnt only too well in the hospital.

But she also discovered that she wanted to be close to Angelo again. Had that first flying experience been a test of courage or rather of love? While on the one hand she was proud of the audacity she had shown, on the other hand she knew she would be sorry if she didn't see Angelo again. She needed to think about it.

Alice sensed that the two of them had completely opposite views on life. He was a young instructor with many dreams, a boy flying in the air in both body and mind, who wanted to experience the third dimension, the vertical one, the most dangerous one, which most people avoid.

She, on the other hand, was a cautious and matter-of-fact woman with a somewhat shy character and her feet firmly placed on the ground. She could never forget what she had been taught since childhood: "It's dangerous ... don't take risks!"

But in her heart of hearts Alice already felt in love with that handsome young man with light eyes, brown hair and the peculiar but nice smile that had fascinated her.

"Perhaps - she found herself reflecting - we could feel good together: we are so different, but maybe for this very reason it could work! We complete each other, in fact. He is spontaneous, he would get along with anyone, to him every person is a source of enrichment. I am more reflective, I tend to keep to myself, before making friends with anyone I want to know them well ... "

And her thoughts flowed, along with a few doubts.

"How many girls has he already taken flying with a paraglider?... it's okay, that's just a weekend job for him, but ... and he's too young for me, maybe he doesn't even think about one like me ... but I have guts, I have proved it ... yet perhaps I had better give up, it could be dangerous, the chances of an accident will increase as I do it again and again –"

Her reflections swayed between hope and uncertainty. She decided to plunge back into her work and try to forget all about it.

One Saturday afternoon Alice was in her garden, hanging out clothes to dry in the sun, when she heard a rustle in the air. It was little more than a gust of wind. She just had time to turn around to catch a shadow sliding swiftly across the lawn. Then she looked up and saw a paraglider landing in her garden.

Still stunned, because no paraglider had ever happened to choose her garden as a landing strip, she immediately thought of an emergency. But the next moment she knew it wasn't. Even before he took off his helmet and glasses she knew, by the characteristic smile she knew so well, that it was Angelo.

"Angelo! What a nice surprise! How did you know I was at home?"

"My binoculars have been focused on your house since this morning! But you never turned up!"

She managed a shy smile.

"Look, next Saturday we are having a baptismal party for the new eagles, and you are invited too. We will meet at the Garden Relais, I would like you to come too, please. At four p.m., write that down!"

At that moment a young girl came out of the house and Alice introduced her to Angelo. "This is my sister Beatrice."

The newcomer held out her hand to him, and

when Angelo shook it she threw a witty joke.

"But then it's true what my sister says!"

He shot her a curious look.

"Why? What does Alice say?"

"Alice argues that angels come down from heaven! Sometimes too hastily!", laughed Beatrice.

Angelo also laughed, while Alice felt a little embarrassed, as if her feelings had been laid bare.

Beatrice was three years younger than Alice. She had a beautiful physique and long dark blond hair that framed two light blue eyes, a magnet for the young man's attention. Apart from the attractive shapes of her body and the clothing that highlighted them, Beatrice also appeared different temperamentally compared to her older sister. She was an instinctive girl, ever ready for new adventures.

Attracted by the loud talking, the two young women's mother came out into the garden too. Alice introduced Angelo as a friend she had met in the hospital. She hadn't mentioned to her mother the flight experience, which, on the other hand, she had revealed to Beatrice. Then she asked the young man if he would like to be driven to the nearby airstrip and he agreed.

When Alice returned home, however, she realized that she could not keep that secret from her mother any longer and told her everything. However, she reassured her by promising that she would never fly again.

But she *would* go to the party she was invited to the following Saturday. Angelo's call was too strong for her to ignore.

Luckily Alice hadn't put on a fancy dress on the Saturday afternoon she went to the paragliding party.

Flight baptisms and carnival were celebrated together. There were those who sprayed sticky foam, those who blew into paper trumpets and those who threw confetti. Angelo had had cardboard wings prepared for the new eagles to wear by tying them behind their shoulders. The ceremony was a lot of fun made up of music, dancing, jokes, pastries and sandwiches accompanied by beer and sparkling wine.

The climax of the party was when Angelo slipped a CD of slow dance into the player and invited Alice to dance. She wasn't expecting anything else. The man asked her if her fear of flying had gone, but she replied that she still did not feel completely safe.

Alice insisted that while working in the hospital she occasionally saw someone taken to the emergency room because he had fallen, and often with worse consequences than those suffered by Angelo.

But the young man calmly answered her with his vision of life.

"Living is in itself a risk, from the moment

you are born. If you looked at the statistics you would see that risks are lower for those who fly than those who wander the streets. Each activity depends on how it is performed and how one is prepared. "

He seemed convinced and also convincing.

"If you carry out all the control operations thoroughly before taking off and don't make reckless maneuvers, risks become very unlikely", concluded Angelo with a smile that tried to be reassuring.

Angelo knew, however, that he was lying about the statistics.

"But I see those who ..."

Alice did not have time to finish the sentence because the man kissed her spontaneously, instinctively. It was what she had been waiting for since she entered that room full of cheering young people.

Angelo drew her to him, stroking her face and brushing her hair away from her forehead. Their mouths joined.

It was a light kiss, which then became more and more passionate as, hugging tightly, they caressed and explored each other in desire.

As their first intimate contact, it was as if they had always known and belonged to each other.

Alice returned his kisses with passion. To the scrupulous nurse it seemed that heaven had indeed sent an angel to give her a pair of wings too.

And she was flying with him, again.

On the Sunday morning after the party Alice looked transformed. Even though the day was a wintry gray, she opened her bedroom windows and began to sing as if spring were inside her. She had played a hit CD from the eighties and sung like she had never done before in her life a song she had listened to so many times when she was a girl, "It's raining men" by the Weather Girls.

At her house they were amazed to see her so cheerful, but they understood why.

It's raining men, hallelujah ... It's raining men ...

Alice's voice spread all over the house.

It's raining men, hallelujah ... It's raining men ...

Not so many men had rained on the young nurse in life, but now one had come down from the sky with a paraglider, and his name was Angelo. An angel just for her.

What she hoped for in her heart had come true, the man had declared himself and kissed her while they danced. By now Alice felt sure of the love that Angelo felt for her, and though she was afraid that something would happen to him in flight, she tried not to think about it

– or at any rate not to blame him for fears that were all her own.

She had never talked to anyone about the nightmares that she occasionally had at night, not even to her mother and sister, let alone Angelo. Yet he somehow sensed her fears and hoped to help her overcome them.

Alice went to mass every Sunday morning and prayed that the sky would protect him; after returning home she put in the "It's raining men" CD and went out into the garden with binoculars to scan the blue vault. She wanted to make sure her angel was flying safely above her house and while he flew, whether for work or play, she felt a little more relaxed if she could keep an eye on him.

Strangely she was calmer at home, when she saw Angelo fluttering in the air, in the situation in which an accident could have happened to him, than when she was at work in the hospital and heard the calls to the emergency room or saw injured people arriving in the ambulance, without knowing where he was or what he was doing at the time.

One day when the weather conditions did not allow flying, Alice suggested she and Angelo take a tour of Bassano, so he would discover the beauties of the city that he had only observed from above when paragliding.

Alice took him to see the wooden *Ponte degli Alpini*, famous all over Italy, designed by the great architect Andrea Palladio and dating back from 1568. As they strolled over the bridge, she asked Angelo if he knew the famous song and he replied in the affirmative. As proof he sang the refrain:

On the Bassano bridge, we will take each other's hand, we will take each other's hand and share a little love kiss
.....

It made her smile to hear those rolled r's of his, and he was also a little out of tune, but she was far more interested in the kiss that came spontaneously from Angelo immediately afterwards.

During the walk the two young people talked about their families and Alice explained that in her house they were all females, because her father had died in an accident when she was a teenager.

However, she did not want to go into details.

Instead, Angelo told her about the incredible meeting between his German mother and his father, an American of Italian origin then serving in the army at the Ederle military base in Vicenza.

They walked around the entire city, turning under the arcades of the Piazza Libertà and then crossing the Piazza Garibaldi, once called "Piazza delle Erbe", as farmers brought their agricultural products there to sell.

Alice showed him, on the north side, the Civic Tower and the church of San Francesco and, on the south side, the Civic Museum.

In 1898 the mayor Bonaguro built a water pipe which, drawing from the wells of the Fontanazzi di Cismon, brought pure spring water to the middle of the main square. The inauguration of the Bonaguro fountain, a sculpture of pink Verona marble by Carlo Spazzi, was an event of national importance at the time.

Then the two lovers bought two bunches of asparagus that farmers of the area sold at their stalls. Alice had asked her mother if she could bring a friend for lunch and asparagus would be the main dish on the menu. On that occasion Alice would introduce Angelo as her boyfriend.

The other bunch of asparagus was for a second lunch at which the young man, in turn, would introduce her to his parents.

46

At Alice's house, Beatrice was missing for lunch, because she had gone for a trip in the mountains with some friends. Beatrice was called Bea in the family. And beautiful – what the word *bea* meant in the local dialect - she really was. Angelo, though of course noticing her absence, said nothing, but it was Alice's mother who explained her absence.

"Always on the move, Bea. That girl is unlikely to ever be found under the roof of this house. A real tramp!" She exclaimed disconsolately. "I think Alice told you that I'm a widow, and that her father has been missing for so many years, since she was little girl," her mother added in a subdued tone.

Angelo, caught a little by surprise, replied briefly that the fact had been mentioned to him. However, he was careful not to ask any questions. He remembered Alice's reluctance to go into details.

After lunch the younger woman was eager to go for a ride. The ground seemed to burn under her feet.

A few hours later, when the two women were alone, Alice's mother did not fail to confess her fears about her daughter's relationship with the paraglider. They were alone at dinner because Beatrice, as usual, was out with friends.

"Alice, you know very well that we love you, but we are afraid that something will happen to you .... it is dangerous to do this flying sport, we don't want to lose you or at any rate live in this anguish. And even if nothing happens to you, you could find yourself a widow one day too! "

Alice listened without speaking, because she already knew about her mother's worries.

"I am already anxious about your sister, who is always around, but by now I have resigned myself to the situation. I hope that at least you have the judgment that your sister lacks ..."

As the elder daughter, Alice had always been considered the one who had to watch over what Beatrice was up to. She had felt the weight of responsibility towards her younger sister since she was a child. Not surprisingly, over time, she had developed a markedly judicious character.

Alice tried to reassure her mother by telling her that she would not be infected by the passion for flying. She knew only too well, from her experience in the emergency room, what were the possible consequences of that kind of sporting activity.

Angelo phoned his parents that he would visit them the following Friday with a friend from Bassano del Grappa.
They would bring them a bunch of asparagus and some eggs.

When the appointed day arrived, it was Angelo's turn to introduce Alice to his parents. She had brought a bottle of grappa for Angelo's father and a bouquet of flowers for his mother.

Alice suggested boiling the asparagus together with the eggs, as is typically done in the Bassano area. The asparagus and eggs would make up the third course. In the meantime, Angelo's mother would prepare rice and peas (*risi e bisi*) as a first course and mixed fried fish as a second. As dessert. they would have *zaeti*, typical Venetian biscuits. Their name comes from the word that in the Venetian dialect means yellow.

While the women were cooking in the kitchen, Angelo and his father went out to make arrangements with a gondolier friend for a gondola ride in the afternoon.

During the preparation of the lunch the two women talked a little to get to know each other.

When Alice said that she worked in a hospital emergency room, and that she saw people involved in many types of accidents, immediately and spontaneously Angelo's mother confessed her fears about her son's passion for flying, as was natural for a mother.

Alice admitted that she had flown only once with Angelo, and it had been very exciting, but she no longer wanted to put herself in danger. Angelo had reassured her that he would never take unnecessary risks or do acrobatic maneuvers with the paraglider. At the same time, she did not feel like obliging Angelo to give up his favorite passion. For now, all she could do was hope for the best.

After the risotto with peas, which was soft and well-creamed, and the Venetian-style mixed frying, it was the turn of the long white asparagus from Bassano, accompanied by a sauce of boiled eggs mashed with oil, salt, pepper and vinegar. The third course was accompanied with very cool prosecco- They ended the lunch in style by munching the *zaeti* with an excellent Moscato *passito*.

The two young people spent the afternoon touring the canals of Venice in a gondola, the gondolier himself also acting as their guide.

They flowed under the Rialto bridge, but then Angelo preferred to go around quieter canals, because the Grand Canal was too busy with *vaporetti* full of tourists and fast motorboats that created annoying wave motions.

It was a carefree day: Angelo wished he could show Alice around all the corners of that city that are unknown to most tourists.

Finally, they concluded it by wandering around the **bàcari**, the small Venetian taverns known only to fishermen and locals, where you could spend several cheerful hours chattering and joking while sipping spritzes and nibbling at fish-based snacks.

Alice's thoughts, however, occasionally returned to what her mother had recommended and to what Angelo's mother had also told her.

A vague and indecisive worry, at a half-conscious level, appeared every now and then in Alice's mind. If they formed a family, and if Angelo became a father, would he change his outlook on life and accept responsibilities? But at that moment she was too happy and didn't feel like questioning the state of things. She was afraid of ruining the magical atmosphere that enveloped them.

The thought of starting a family, however, continued to occasionally emerge from the waves of her unconscious. She did everything to drown it and threw herself into Angelo's arms to try to make him happy, with all the love she could give him in both soul and body.

For them it was a period of fiery and unreserved love. Then, like a bolt out of the blue, the suspicion of being pregnant came to disturb Alice's magical moment. Before talking to Angelo she wanted to be sure: she took the test twice with the kits purchased at the pharmacy, which confirmed her suspicions.

Alice thought about what could be the right occasion to talk about it and how she could introduce solid arguments that would change Angelo's attitude towards life.

"Fatherhood should help him feel more responsible and be more careful about putting his life at risk," she kept thinking to herself.

She waited for the right moment to tell Angelo that he would be a father and the opportunity came one evening when they went out for a pizza. Alice began the conversation by beating about the bush for a while.

"Angelo, how are the flying courses going? Are there are new people? And new girls?"

She threw in the questions, smiling casually at him.

"As usual, more or less. Why are you asking me? Are you jealous?" he answered smiling back.

"Honestly I have to tell you that seeing so many women around you doesn't make me happy, but I understand that this is your job and your passion ... but you never know!", she continued.

Then, smiling, she added: "Do you think that one day, when we get married, this could be your job even if you have, maybe, children? I mean ... can this job be safe enough to start a family?"

53

Alice was getting to the heart of the matter.

Angelo looked at her with some curiosity, trying to figure out if her questions were aiming at anything particular.

"Are you trying to tell me that you want us to get married? Or that mine isn't a stable and safe job for one who means to get married? Maybe you don't trust me and want to put a stop to our relationship?" he inquired looking into her eyes.   "Are you not happy with this situation of freedom that we are in? Do you feel insecure? Now we are free from commitments with others, free as when I am up there in the sky!"

Angelo paused briefly and then resumed.

"I understand, come on. You are not sure of my love and want us to get married. Isn't that so?"

"Why not? If I asked you to marry me, wouldn't it suit you?", she retorted a little annoyed.

"I love you and in principle I would marry you, wouldn't I! But at the moment I'm not ready yet, flying school is not a real job, it goes a little bit in periods, you know. I'm sure we'd better think about it a little longer, hadn't we? ", Angelo suggested. "After all we are still young, we still have a lot of time ahead!"

54

Alice gave a long sigh.

"Suppose it could happen, by chance, that I get pregnant .... what would you advise me to do in that case? At any rate, what would *you* do

Angelo was surprised and suddenly became serious.

"Are you telling me ... that you are ..."

He couldn't finish the sentence.

"Yes! I'm telling you that I'm pregnant, Angelo! But maybe this is not the right time for you, is it?", Alice snapped, scared at the answer she could receive.

Angelo looked like a pugilist who has been punched squarely in the face. His eyes were wide open and he managed to ask a single question.

"Are you sure?

"Of course I'm sure, I took the test twice! Unfortunately I have irregular menstruation and this, perhaps, has complicated things ... But you don't seem very happy with this news ... indeed, maybe you are sorry ... "

Angelo tried to save face: "I'm not sorry, Alice, but maybe this isn't the best time to start a family. If that's what you want, I'm ready ... but we should both to think about it

... let's think about it a little longer, shall we?"

Alice had hoped for a different reaction from him and the evening at the pizzeria ended sadly. Angelo barely managed to finish his now cold pizza. Now he had one more thought to go to bed with.

Alice, on the other hand, had two thoughts on her mind: on the one hand she was wondering what could happen to Angelo during the next flight, on the other hand she was thinking about the birth of a baby whose father was not yet ready to be a father.

She knew how difficult it was to ask Angelo to give up his passion for flying. She sensed what he must feel when he flew, because she had experienced that intoxicating feeling of freedom too. It was obvious that to Angelo her motherhood seemed like a stumbling block in his way, a trick of fate, almost a bottleneck that she was forcing him to go through.

After that evening their relationship went on in phases of light and shadow for some time. Angelo continued to fly in the sky and Alice to navigate in her fears. Each time she looked forward to the evening when she would see her lover safe on the ground again.

It was a windy Sunday morning in late spring. After mass, Alice had returned to her home with the beautiful garden and was deciding whether or not to turn on the CD player to listen to some music and relax a bit while she prepare food.

At that moment she heard a gust of wind coming from outside, followed by a thunderous noise of broken branches and accompanied by a groan.

She ran out into the garden to see what had happened and found herself in front of a man lying unconscious on the ground.

At first she did not understand, but then, seeing a large colored parachute near that man half covered in branches and leaves, she realized that it was a fallen paraglider.

For the second time someone was raining from the sky directly into her garden, but this time the situation was completely different.

Alice felt her heart beat so hard that she could feel it in her throat.

She was frozen for a moment, fearing that it was Angelo, but after realizing that that was not the case she ran towards the unfortunate paraglider.

Her mind, automatically, began to

implement the operations she had learned in the various activities performed in the emergency room. Like the expert nurse she was, she checked for heartbeat and breathing and practiced all the maneuvers necessary to try to save the man's life, starting with mouth-to-mouth respiration and heart massage.

In the meantime she had called 112, which often intervened in the area for the poor wretches who fell.

The wounded man was rushed to hospital in an ambulance with its siren blaring – a sound which, as usual, caused a lump in her throat.

Unluckily, the man did not make it: he had to undergo several operations to reduce fractures, but the complications were fatal.

That incident, experienced in the first person, deeply disturbed the young woman, who on that same evening decided it was time for a showdown with Angelo.

58

When they met again after the dramatic episode, Angelo noticed that there must be something wrong. Alice returned his greeting in an unusually laconic way and he sensed that tonight would not be like all the other times. He then asked the young woman to give him an explanation for that sullen face.

Alice told him about what had happened right in the garden of her house, with the fall of the paraglider, to whom she herself had given immediate aid.

Angelo told her he hadn't heard anything about that, but Alice suspected that he was only too well informed about the tragic event: certain news circulated quickly in the paragliding milieu.

"I'm afraid, Angelo, that this could happen to you one day too!", She said sadly, and then, continuing more decisively: "I can't go on like this anymore, with the terror that it could happen to the person I love most of all! "

"It has already happened to me, you know, but you saw that I had protected myself with the emergency parachute. True, I made a little mistake, I underestimated the danger. But it will never happen again, I promise!"

Their tempers heated up, as did their tones,

but Angelo was still trying to joke.

"It will never happen to me because I'm an angel, you know ..."

"Your name is Angelo, but you don't have wings ... and I don't want to think of myself as a future widow or, even worse, as a caregiver for someone who will be ruined for life!"

"Death does not exist as an entity!", Angelo ruled.

"What are you saying? You always want to joke, even when there is nothing to joke about! I saw my father die before my eyes when I was a child ... even now I have nightmares from time to time. I see my father die in front of me after a fall from a paraglider! I said my father, because I know the man in the dream is my father – but he has your face!"

"Wait. I want you to think about this a little bit," Angelo replied. "Have you ever seen death in person? Can you describe it to me? Or do you know anyone who has ever seen it?"

"I see people die in the hospital!" Alice replied, but she was unable to stop Angelo's retorts.

"It was once imagined that death was an entity represented by a skeleton with a scythe that carried away people, both good and bad. It hit the predestined as a deity could, a kind of rival of that other deity who gave life. ... "

The guy persisted with his philosophical outlook on life.

"If a child builds a sand castle and then the tide destroys it in the evening, what would you say? That it was struck by death? No! You would say that it is only a change in shape or state of matter, like snow melting in the sun! "

Alice stared at him silently.

"In the same way, when a baby is born it weighs a few kilos, and then swallows up matter until it reaches the weight of an adult. But even if it is in good health, that human being begins to degrade in an aging process that leads to a change of state and form. All we are is matter, all we do is change forms, whatever religion or society may tell us."

Then, suddenly, Angelo fell silent too.

He understood that he was treading on soft ground and tried other arguments.

"If you want to impose your own views on me right now, just imagine what would happen after we got married! Instead, you should share with me the things I like ... maybe we'd better focus on our different backgrounds.

"No, it is you who are selfish! You think only of yourself, you are not capable of giving up anything for love! Maybe I had better consider having an abortion, as it would be a burden for you to have to marry me too. Yes, we both had better reflect on our past.

Angelo felt that Alice had hit the mark, and did not reply to that. But he still had something to complain about.

"You can't ask me to give up what is my greatest passion. In love you can't just ask, you must also give, and then you knew what I would do! But yes, I will find other girls, more courageous than you! Indeed, I wonder how you manage to work in the emergency room with all the fears you have!

But she wasn't finished yet, either.

"I get a lump in my throat when I hear the ambulances, it's true, luckily they turn off the siren near the hospital ... and from that moment I know I have to do all I can to help those who are sick ... As for the rest, of course in love one must give and can't just ask! But how can I live with a man who puts his life at risk every week? A boy with his head still in the clouds! You are just incapable of giving up! ", she yelled in his face.

Then she turned and went out slamming the door.

For Alice it was one of the saddest times of her life. Her pain was noticed by everyone, both in the hospital and at home. She herself realized that something inside her had changed for the worse. She had become impatient, reacted with impulsive outbursts that made her unpleasant in the eyes of her colleagues.

Then, in the crucial moments of her work in the hospital, she experienced sudden bumps of pelvic pain and small vaginal bleeding.

She went to her family doctor, who advised her to take a few days' rest to see if it was a passing thing or a possible miscarriage.

This forced her to stay at home for a few days, until the symptoms gradually waned.

Her relationship with Angelo had loosened to the point that by now they saw each other occasionally on the weekend at the landing field, their mutual recognition reduced to mere exchanges of greetings.

After about a month Alice noticed that her periods had resumed and this made her sorry.

She had wanted a child from Angelo, marriage or no marriage. Because that was the great love of her life, even if this love was beginning to take on a different connotation from what she had initially imagined.

When she told Angelo she tried to make him understand how sorry she was and he was very kind at that juncture. He held her in his arms and kissing her forehead whispered: "Don't worry, you'll see that we will make up for what we have lost."

Alice looked Angelo in the eyes and thought she saw a softening of his face.

"Maybe he's right", she thought. "Perhaps it is still too early to think about starting a family, after all we have been together for such a short time". And she herself took the initiative of suggesting a pause in their relationship. Angelo agreed. The spell was now broken, their love shattered like a broken vase.

So Angelo slowly slipped out of Alice's life, and was free to fly.

Over the next few days Alice kept checking the paragliders flying over her garden, hoping Angelo would miss her more than she missed him. But neither of them wanted to give in.

This situation went on like that for most of the summer, with her spying on him with binoculars and Angelo occasionally glancing at Alice's house from the paraglider.

One day, however, Alice, who could no longer hold on, decided to board the car and drive to the runway. It had been a few days since she had last seen Angelo's paraglider flying over her home and she felt anxious.

She found Luca, Angelo's flight school partner, and asked him if he knew where he was. He replied that Angelo was at the flying field with clients for the first paragliding lessons and, if she liked, he would tell him that she was looking for him. Alice replied that it was not needed, that it was not really important.

Then, once she got into the car and left, she remembered where the flying field was, that is, a few kilometers from the take-off runway towards the top of the mountain. She changed her mind and headed for the place.

The pitch is nothing more than a slightly

sloping grassy stretch, where the aspiring flyers take their early flight tests hanging from the paraglider at the height of one or two meters at most and for the length of a few tens of meters, assisted by the advice of their instructor. Basically, a series of jumps of increasing lengths.

She stopped the car a short way before the bend, got out of the car and walked as far as the bush right at the bend. As she stood behind it she could see the area above without being seen.

Angelo was giving explanations about paragliding to young people around him. A blonde girl was hidden behind him. When the latter moved to point to something, Alice was surprised to see that it was Beatrice. Angelo was speaking to all the young people present, but to Alice it seemed that between him and her sister there was something beyond the normal relationships between instructor and pupil.

They laughed and joked, they seemed very close. Then Angelo put his arm over Beatrice's shoulder and finally hugged her. Alice didn't want to see anything else.

She had an impulse to leap out of the bush in a rage and run to ask for an explanation. But an explanation of what? Wasn't her sister free to do paragliding? Wasn't it her own jealousy that was to blame?

It probably was.

Beatrice, the one who never wanted to give up anything! Even as a child it was always Alice who gave in in disputes over toys. She was older than Bea and was supposed to be more understanding, more judicious. Or so her parents had taught her.

That time was now long gone, each of them made their own choices, had their own friendships, their own stories, though there still was a little intimacy left between them. Why hadn't Beatrice talked about that with her? Angelo was not a doll that Alice had to compete for with Beatrice.

At that moment when her consciousness was clouded, Alice saw her sister as a potential rival, a kind of praying mantis.

The female praying mantis is an insect that mates with the male and once it is no longer needed devours it.

In the same way Beatrice fascinated boys in order to use them for what she wanted to obtain, and when it seemed to her she no longer needed them, she just dropped them.

These thoughts crossed Alice's mind, but then her shy nature had the upper hand and she walked away silently. Se would wait for another occasion and see how they would justify themselves.

She got back into the car, started the engine and took the road home.

She had understood one thing: it cost her a lot to be without Angelo, whereas he seemed to be doing well enough without her. Indeed, apparently he had already found someone to replace her.

The next day it was Angelo who phoned Alice. He had been informed of her visit by his partner Luca.

The two former lovers met that evening to talk to each other in the same pizzeria near the landing strip.

Alice was determined not to lose the challenge against Beatrice. She wanted to try to get back what she thought was hers.

She would try to glue together the shards of that pot that had been shattered.

After they said hello to each other coldly, Angelo asked her what was the reason for her visit the previous day, which had been reported to him by Luca.

"I came to see if we could somehow try to get back together", Alice explained, "but then I realized that you are fine even without me, and that you are always in good company, so I gave it up", she concluded ironically.

"You know very well that this is my job and that I have to be nice to clients. Since you met me you have known this is my passion. I suspect yours is just jealousy," he replied.

Angelo paused for a moment and then continued: "Yes, I really think that you can't bear the idea of seeing me in the company of other women, and your fear of flight accidents is just an excuse," he finally blurted out.

Angelo's tone was rising, but she wasn't going to just listen to him.

"You're wrong, I'm not afraid to compete against other women, I can defend myself on equal terms. But it is against death that I cannot fight".

"I've already told you what I think about death."

"Angelo, I've checked the statistics about the risks of those who paraglide, disclosed by one who practices it. It is one of the riskiest sports! It is more dangerous than mountaineering in Nepal, than bungee jumping or parachuting, more than any other activity! "

Alice was like a river in flood.

"You know I work in the ER, and thanks to that I realize how many people risk their safety in such a stupid way. Every time I hear an ambulance getting in I'm afraid it's you! Life is not about wanting to get it all immediately for fear that tomorrow may be too late ... life is a project to be built day by day. You cannot become a father and the next day throw yourself off a cliff to experience strong emotions! Risk, emotions, intoxication lead one to addiction and addiction to adrenaline and in the long run even to the likelihood of death. Paunchy office workers are offered adventurous tours in dangerous countries, extreme climbs, bungee jumping sessions. Cheaper and cheaper, lighter and lighter paragliders are sold ... and you get caught up in the whirlwind of consumerism. "

Angelo did not give her time to continue her fervent peroration.

"What would you like me to do? Leave this one pleasure I have, leave my partner to fend for himself? Would you force me to live in a two-dimensional world? I feel free only when I'm up there, high in the sky, caressing the clouds! I really don't understand you, Alice ... women who are friends of other paragliding pilots are not as anxious as you. No airplane pilot would have a wife if all women were the same as you! Why are you so different? When you met me I was like that, and I still am. I'm sorry for you, Alice. Bye. "

Angelo turned his back on the girl and went away leaving her distraught.

Alice hadn't had time to talk about Beatrice's presence at the flying field, but perhaps she wouldn't have mentioned it anyway, she was too angry about that.

She was convinced that one of the reasons why Angelo had turned away from her, and not the slightest one, was her sister.

After that unhappy conversation the two of them went back to their separate lives.

After high school, Beatrice had gotten a degree in economics in Italy and then a master's degree in England. Traveling the world was one of her aspirations in life. Among her friends were some American young people and Bea, with her good English, aimed at a future in the United States.

When she met Angelo she had thought of taking her American friends to do some flying, in order to further strengthen relations with them.

So one day she showed up at the take-off field with a group of young men and women.

Angelo felt very much attracted to Beatrice and in exchange for her favor of bringing him customers he was all smiles and hugs.

Then Bea asked him to be allowed to fly too, which Angelo gladly granted her.

It was just as the relationship between Angelo and Alice was cracking that Beatrice began to take up more and more space in Angelo's thoughts.

One evening, when Alice was on duty in the hospital, her sister and Angelo found themselves in the brewery talking about that ambiguous situation.

After a couple of beers Angelo confessed to Bea that his relationship with Alice was practically over.

"We are like day and night, we will never get along. She would like me to give up flying, but to me flying is life!" Angelo said disconsolately.

Beatrice tried to advise him to wait, as she knew that Alice tended to become compliant with the passing of time.

When they got out of the brewery and into his car, In the intimacy that had formed between them, Bea, as if soothingly, touched his hand on the steering wheel.

"If I had known you before ... you would have been the right woman for me ... a woman who wants to live life intensely, like me ...", he whispered to her, and while Beatrice held his hand Angelo drew nearer and kissed her on the lips. But the girl withdrew instinctively.

She liked Angelo a lot, and perhaps if he had insisted Bea would have given in. But that was not the right time. Alice had always trusted her, and Beatrice didn't feel like taking advantage of her sister's critical situation.

She couldn't, after trying to console her, betray her like that, stab her in the back.

Maybe one day, when the feelings had

cleared up with a definite solution, it would be different.

At the same time she did not know how to express to Angelo the depth of the fears that tormented Alice.

Angelo felt that Beatrice had become stiff and apologized.

"Sorry, I don't know what got me. Maybe it's the beer's fault. Now I'll take you home."

Beatrice smiled at him and removed her hand from Angelo's. He started the car and they left for her home.

Alice tried to plunge into work in an attempt to forget all about Angelo and his firm intention not to renounce that exciting but risky sport.

She also waited to see the development of his suspected affair with Beatrice.

Alice had come to the conclusion that perhaps it was right to leave the field open to her sister. It would be better for both Angelo and herself if he and Beatrice happy and well together.

Perhaps his sister was better suited than her to getting along with that man.

The only one not to feel guilty at all was Alice's mother, as she had advised her daughter not to practice such a dangerous sport or to associate with people with that passion.

She felt that a juvenile disappointment today was better than a probable widowhood tomorrow.

But the very job Alice did could hardly help her forget Angelo. Especially when injured people were taken into the emergency room as a consequence of flight accidents, her thoughts immediately flew to her ex-boyfriend.

Alice's colleagues had noticed the sadness in the eyes of that young woman, who had been looking shy and taciturn since her return.

The same happened at home, where she no longer spoke to Bea. It was as if a wall had risen between the two sisters.

To all this was added the story that Angelo's mother had told Alice about George, her husband.

Angelo's father had also been a daredevil, he had practiced many sports, all of them quite dangerous.

As a young man, besides being a US Army paratrooper, he owned a powerful motorcycle.

One day a car had suddenly crossed his way in an attempt to turn into a side road, but it hadn't completed the maneuver and had stopped abruptly in the middle of the main road as his motorcycle was rushing past it. Unable to avoid the obstacle, George crashed into the nose of the car, flying over its hood. Luck would have it that he had on a helmet and landed butt first on a flowerbed. The motorcycle was destroyed, but the only physical damage to George was a blueish butt which George exhibited at the seaside that summer from under his swimsuit.

Many other times he had been involved in

cycling accidents caused by careless motorists. In short, several parts of George's body bore the marks of his adventures: a finger of his left hand and his left collarbone had broken, he had various scars here and there, his tongue had been stitched up and a few teeth had been replaced.

Yet, despite all his motorcycling, road cycling, ski mountaineering and climbing, he had always managed to get out of it alive and kicking.

Since Angelo was a child, his father had accustomed him to not being afraid of voids: he often threw him in the air and then caught him as he fell. Or he would take him on the most dangerous rides in amusement parks, even on roller coasters.

In short, as Angelo grew up he seemed to have developed no fear of danger. Or, maybe, he just felt he had to prove to his dad that he was like him.

George was probably a myth for Angelo.

And the son seemed to think that he too was under the wing of fate.

One Saturday in early autumn, while Alice was on duty in another unit of the hospital, she heard that an injured person had arrived in the emergency room unconscious from a paragliding fall.

The man had multiple fractures, facial trauma and a probable spinal cord injury.

When she realized it was Angelo, Alice fainted and a fellow nurse had to look after her too. Once she regained consciousness, she plucked up courage and asked to go and see him in person.

Angelo had been taken to the post anesthesia room before being transferred to the intensive care unit. In anger, she wanted to slap him or choke him with her hands, but she checked herself and only a few tears came out.

After he woke up, as soon as she could she went to see him. She comforted him and looked after him with kindness, but neither of them dared to mention the flight.

It would have been easy for her now to say "I told you".

Alice talked about what had happened to Angelo at home too.

One reason she did so was her eagerness to see Beatrice's reaction, as a way to find out how things stood between Angelo and her sister.

She was therefore surprised to notice that Beatrice was certainly sorry, but by no means in despair. It was also clear that she hadn't heard about the accident before. Which meant she hadn't seen Angelo for a while.

During the period of hospitalization, Alice was always beside Angelo. Whatever he needed, he knew he could count on her. Beatrice, on the other hand, only came to see the young man in the hospital once.

Her visit did not last as long as half an hour, and she brought him a book as a gift.

Something must have gone wrong between them, Alice thought. She knew that Beatrice had been quick to dump her previous boyfriends.

But, after all, between Beatrice and Angelo there might have been nothing, or, if there had been anything, it had been soon over.

This doubt remained with her for quite some time, but she dared not ask either of them to solve it.

After two months of treatment in hospital, the doctors discharged Angelo with a bleak prognosis: paraplegia, that is, the impossibility of walking. Angelo did not show any strong feelings, but by now he was resigned to using a wheelchair for life. To Alice, who looked at him intently, he seemed like another man, the bravado had disappeared from the young face she knew so well.

On the day of Angelo's discharge from hospital his parents were there and so was Alice. The young man asked her to take him where they could be alone for a moment and then took her hands in his and kissed them.

"Alice, you have been my angel in these days of hell for you and me, but I have no right to drag you into this pain. You deserve a man who can make you happy... I will thank you forever, but we had better break up permanently. You...you must leave me!You were right when you advised me to leave that risky sport "

Alice smiled at him. She was moved.
"I have something to tell you, Angelo, and I hope you understand. I talked to your parents and we agreed that I will take care of you at your house in Venice. I will be the one to oversee your rehabilitation, there are new

treatments in this field and you'll see that we'll have you walking again! ", she replied enthusiastically.

"No, Alice, I'll never walk again, let's not delude ourselves. The wheelchair is my future, and I'll never walk or fly anymore, forever!"

"Please, let me tempt you! And then I have one more thing to tell you ... I have already applied to quit my job in the hospital, In fact I resigned a month ago. The doctors understood my decision to follow you and your parents agree too."

An even bigger smile appeared on the girl's face.

"Now you can't leave me in trouble, I will be paid by your family, so if I'm not up to my new job you can fire me!"

Angelo gave a long sigh.

"Okay Alice, I've done a lot of stupid things, and now you have the right to do one too, so we're even."

Angelo, who knew Venice, imagined how difficult life would be for a person confined on a wheelchair, but also for the one who would have to push it.

"With over 400 bridges, built for those with good legs and good arms, she will soon get tired and think again about the life that awaits her", he kept repeating to himself.

Angelo's parents left the Venice apartment and moved to their home in Bolzano.

They preferred the mountains in winter, or so they said.

Angelo's father had retired from military engagements some years before, and his mother devoted herself almost full time to her favorite passion, landscape painting:

"At least my landscapes will change a bit!", was her amused comment.

Alice's mother agreed with a sigh that her daughter would move to Venice, although she was a little sorry to be alone.

But as she was retired and free from commitments too, she would take advantage of the opportunity to visit the lagoon city more often.

So the two young people went to live in Venice. There was initially a period of necessary adjustment to their life together, but then things took on a daily routine of their own.

In the morning, once the housework was sorted out, they went shopping together.

After lunch Alice took Angelo for a walk, during which he introduced her to his fishing friends, who were always ready for jokes when they saw them.

"Angelo, tell the truth, it's you who found

an angel this time!" Mario shouted to him and Bepi added: "I think he did it right to throw himself down!"

One of the first walks they took was naturally bound for the Piazza San Marco.

Fortunately, the queue to climb the bell tower was reasonably short that day. They reached the top by lift: the view was spectacular, you could see not only all of Venice with its lagoon, but also the mainland and mountains of the Veneto.

Another day was devoted to visiting the Basilica of San Marco, with all the treasures that tourists can admire inside, and the Doge's Palace,

And so, day after day, they went sightseeing in the most beautiful places in Venice. Alice did not tire of pushing the wheelchair up and down the bridges of the city. Angelo, on the other hand, deep down hoped that sooner or later she would feel she had had enough.

Alice saw that through her loving care, constant massage and sensory stimulation, something was improving, though not as quickly as she had been hoping. But she didn't give up.

One day she knelt in front of Angelo, who was sitting on the bed, and asked him if he wanted to go for a walk.

Her request was accompanied by a number of loving kisses, to convince him to leave.

Initially Angelo seemed reluctant, but Alice's insistent and continuous pampering had the effect desired by the girl.

When Alice noticed the sexual arousal she had caused in Angelo, she smiled a winking smile.

"Do you know what? Today I will not let you take the usual stroll in the wheel chair up and down the bridges and streets, no! Today I will let you fly, and without a paraglider!"

She helped him lie down and they spent the whole morning in bed, doing what young lovers do.

Alice was showing him that he could really fly even without wings.

"And if this were not enough for you, you will see that at carnival I will make you fly from the bell tower of San Marco, the flight of the Angel!"

The enterprising nurse and lover laughed again, thinking about the ceremony during which every year at carnival the winner of a beauty contest lets herself down the bell tower of San Marco, attached to a rope, to reach the top of the Doge's Palace.

At this joke, Angelo burst into sincere laughter too.

Those were beautiful days for Alice, and for Angelo it was a period of growing serenity.

But despite the gymnastics and massages, which many times ended up as love sessions, his condition was not improving much.

One day Angelo's mother arrived in Venice and when she was alone with Alice she told her that there were new chances of treatment with electrical stimulation of the spinal cord. For Angelo to be given those treatments, which were still at an experimental level, they would have to go to Switzerland, but since the young man was strongly persuaded that his destiny was already sealed, Alice had, once again, to make him change his mind.

The young woman got ready for the new battle, determined to persuade Angelo to at least give it a try.

In a moment of intimacy Angelo had told Alice that as a child he had received a Lima model train as a gift and his boy's fancy had traveled on that little train all over the world.

On that basis Alice had concocted a plan to surprise Angelo.

One day, as they were recalling that childhood memory, she pretended she had just discovered, by chance, the existence of the famous treatments, which were performed in Lausanne, Switzerland.

"My Angel, would you give me a birthday present?"

"Of course Alice, as long as you don't ask me to run!" He joked.

"I would like to take a trip to Switzerland!"

"What do you want to see in Switzerland? You know there are so many mountains, you'd always have to push the wheelchair up! Unless you want to throw me off some cliff!", he continued jokingly.

"Quiet, my love, if I had wanted to get rid of you I could have done it already here in Venice. With all the water there is round here, a night walk would have been enough and then ... splash, down in the canal ... it would have been simple!", she replied wisely.

And she burst into amused laughter.

"Listen ... I would like to go to Switzerland and listen to what they tell me in this clinic." And she explained what it was. "They seem to have developed advanced treatment for paraplegia! Let's go over there and see. I

87

promise you that if they aren't convincing, I won't ask you for any more attempts."

The request was made in a pleading but sincerely heartfelt tone. As Angelo kept silent, Alice tried to insist.

"Please! I promise you ... I will never ask you for more attempts, this is the last!"

Alice was on her knees looking at him with eyes full of sincere love.

When she wanted something, she could be convincing.

Angelo agreed. He realized that Alice was becoming more and more important in his life.

Alice took care of everything: she booked the hotels and bought the tickets they would need. She also prepared to be the driver in the hired car, one of those low-floored cars designed for wheelchairs.

And so they went to Switzerland.

On the day they arrived at the clinic they had an introductory interview and handed over to the head doctor all the medical documents that had been made available to them by the Italian doctors..

The treatment methods used and the results obtained were presented to the two young people, along with the expenses that were estimated and the presumable recovery times they faced.

During the first few days Angelo would have to undergo further tests, then the head doctor would analyze the results and consult with his medical colleagues.

So they found themselves with a few days available for touring the area.

Alice convinced Angelo that the first day on which he would be free from clinical exams would be spent taking a beautiful ride on the Bernina red train.

Angelo was a little surprised by Alice's request, but eventually he was persuaded that it was better to visit Switzerland than sit still and wait.

Alice immediately picked up the phone to arrange the tour, inquiring about timetables and departure stations and booking seats in the disabled carriage.

On the appointed day they drove back towards Lake Maggiore and Como, and then up to Tirano.

Alice wanted to see once again the lake made famous by the **Promessi Sposi.**

In Tirano they got into a carriage with panoramic windows. The red train started from the Italian station, at 430 meters above sea level, and went to Saint Moritz in Switzerland, at over 1700 meters, then higher still, over the Bernina pass – at an altitude of two thousand two hundred and fifty meters, among snow-capped mountains. The complete 61-kilometer journey lasted two and a half hours.

Luckily Alice had remembered to bring her camera and Angelo was able to take numerous photos of the splendid views.

He was happy and it seemed to him as if he was back in his childhood, when in his fancy he imagined himself traveling all over the world in his miniature train.

The landscape of the snow-capped mountains, admired from inside the train, in the warmth of the panoramic carriage, was truly spectacular.

Alice was fulfilling one of her favorite dreams, which, taken up as she had been by her daily caring routine, she had almost forgotten.

After that adventure, they went to the

90

Jungfrau in the Bern Alps over the weekend.

They spent the night at a hotel in Interlaken. Early in the morrow they left the Interlaken Oststation and after e few stops they arrived at the Kleine Scheidegg station, over two thousand meters above sea level, where they had lunch.

Then they continued on the cogwheel train across the glacial landscape of the Jungfrau and through a seven-kilometer tunnel in the north face of the Eiger.

Once on the Jungfraujoch, they discovered a magnificent high-altitude world made of ice, snow and rock. It is the highest railway station in Europe, 3471 meters above sea level: from there you can go up another 100 meters via a fast lift to the "Sphinx" viewing platform.

Not even with his paraglider had Angelo risen to such altitudes. The building consists of a glass and steel structure that houses an astronomical observatory and a meteorological station. From there they enjoyed a breathtaking view of the Jungfrau and Aletsch glaciers: it was an opportunity to take more fascinating photographs.

The following morning they had to go back to the clinic to begin treatment for Angelo.

Over the following days they found themselves having to follow the institute's strict therapy rules.

At least four days a week he was engaged in rehabilitation, with taxing gymnastics sessions and treatment with electrical stimulation, aimed to reactivate the broken connections between the brain and the muscles.

What with exercises in the gym with special machines designed for that type of injury, and exercises performed in the swimming pool, the days went by very quickly.

In the final rehabilitation period, an exoskeleton was prepared which, through certain orders of the brain, helped Angelo to control the muscles of the legs.

As a matter of fact, the Lausanne institute was researching into the radio transmission of brain impulses to the disconnected parts of the spinal cord: they were at the forefront in this field.

Once he had reached the last phase of the treatment, Angelo was able to walk by standing on two parallel bars along a path whose correctness was constantly kept under control.

After two months he was walking with crutches, and he was recommended to continue the rehabilitation exercises in Italy as well.

At the end of the treatment period he was allowed to keep his pair of crutches as a reward for his perseverance and determination.

Angelo was once again enabling himself for life.

When they returned from Switzerland, after a few months, Angelo was still using crutches, but after another three months of rehabilitative gymnastics he was able to walk on just his legs again. It was not exactly the same as before, he advanced with an effort that made him soon exhausted, but he was walking.

For Alice it was a period of lightheartedness and happiness, which turned into triumph when, in the spring, Angelo, asked her to marry him.

Meanwhile Beatrice had found a job abroad and had been away from home for many months. She had moved to the United States shortly after Angelo's accident.

Alice had never asked her if there was anything between her and Angelo. She simply hoped her suspicions had been wrong, even though her jealousy and fears hadn't completely evaporated.

It was time to prepare all that was necessary for the event. Each of them made out their separate lists of guests

This was an opportunity that Alice did not want to miss.

"Angelo, should we invite Beatrice too?"

"Why not? She's your sister! Besides, she's

always been so kind ... Just think that she even took care of getting me clients by taking her friends to the flying field. Unless she's busy with work, of course. And unless the flight back takes too long..."

Angelo had seemed very natural in his response.

"Okay, I'll try asking her if she can come home by that date," Alice finally replied.

Meanwhile she thought that Angelo's words explained Bea's presence at the flying field.

It suddenly seemed to Alice that a light breath had swept away her doubts, as the wind blows away the clouds and carries them for a ride across the sky.

The ceremony took place in the church of the bride's town. Angelo's father offered to accompany Alice to the altar.

The guests in their cars followed the bride's carriage, pulled by a pair of white horses, which took her to the holy building.

There the bridegroom was waiting, with the priest and the best man, his friend and partner Luca.

Several friends of Angelo's had landed with their paragliders from the nearby mountain.

The officiant, known as the **flying priest**, was a friend of the paragliders, who often went to see him to ask for protection.

The wedding lunch took place in the courtyard of an old farmhouse that had been made into a restaurant.

On the one hand, a table had been set up with appetizers and buffets accompanied by spritzes and other drinks.

On two other tables the guests could choose between the two different menus of the wedding banquet.

During the lunch, Angelo's friends sang the famous Modugno song, with a slight modification: **flying oh, oh ... gliding oh, oh ... in the blue painted of blue ...**

The wedding day ended in an atmosphere of authentic celebration, then the couple happily waved goodbye to the guests and left for their honeymoon, which was a time of lightheartedness and passion.

But then, as time went by, the days of euphoria slowly faded away.

Immediately after the wedding Alice and Angelo returned to live in Venice, but later moved to a new home near Bassano del Grappa.

It was summer and Alice had resumed her former work in the hospital emergency room.

Angelo was enjoying himself with a new interest, gardening, but he often found himself looking up at the sky, watching the paragliders.

A feeling of melancholy kept growming his soul.

Alice too felt a sort of melancholy, albeit originating from a different situation.

There had been an important absence at the wedding: from the United States her sister Beatrice had let her know that she had mandatory business commitments. She had duly wished the newlyweds all happiness.

"Bea has not changed a bit," Alice was still mulling weeks later. "Just at the time when I would have liked to have her here, close to me, now that I feel at peace with her, that I no longer suspect her, she has not shown up".

Bea's had seemed to her almost like an excuse.

Alice couldn't help thinking that maybe she really had something to hide and didn't want to confront her.

One day, before Angelo's accident, Beatrice's mother had taken her aside to talk to her.

"Bea, I suspect that there is an affair between you and Angelo and that Alice is suffering a lot because of it."

"I know, mum ... if I had wanted to, I would have taken Angelo away from Alice ... but the fault is not mine, it is Alice who goes against Angelo and would like him to quit flying. Instead she should accept him for what he is and does. "

"I think Alice is very much in love with Angelo and is afraid of losing him in a flight accident. You don't remember how your father died ... no, you can't remember him, but Alice perhaps feels it was her fault."

The mother had let out a long sigh before resuming her story.

"Alice was playing with her kite, but at one point it got entangled in the branches of a tree. It was to free the kite that your father climbed a ladder ... from which he then fell. When I realized what had happened I found Alice motionless, she was like a marble statue blocked by fear. Maybe she felt responsible, even if I have always tried not to make her feel guilty and not to remind her, but ... I'm afraid that that scene has never left her mind."

In fact Bea's mother was not explaining but rather pleading with her younger daughter.

"Alice was always compliant with you when you were little girls, she let you have her toys, she kept an eye on you and took care you didn't get hurt, and when I was away at work she was like a little daddy for you. You could now reciprocate the love that was given you! "

What Beatrice did not know was that Alice, in moments of despair, wished she could share her fears and nightmares with her sister.

But something stopped her, she was terrified to dig too deep into her own consciousness.

Alice, in fact, had been feeling guilty since she had stood motionless as a child in front of her dying father who had just fallen from that cursed tree.

She was frozen, literally frozen, she didn't know how to help him. If only she had been allowed to, she would have gotten into the ambulance that carried Dad away with blaring sirens.

Alice felt as if she had made an unforgivable mistake, and her father's death was like a stain in her soul.

At that terrible moment she was alone with her father: her little sister Bea was with her mother in another part of the house.

It would have been enough for her to scream or call for help, but instead she was frozen by the fear of being blamed for the fall.

And when she grew up, the underlying guilt feeling filled her with anguish whenever she heard an ambulance siren or she thought that someone she loved might fall from above and leave her alone again.

Beatrice had found herself in a very uncomfortable position: on the one hand was Angelo, whom she liked, and on the other hand was the suffering she would have caused Alice if she had started an affair with him.

But there was a third aspect: bonding with Angelo would compromise her plans to travel the world.

During that time of indecision she had continued to see Angelo secretly.

But then, one day, she made up her mind and got in touch with a friend in the United States, asking him if there were any chances for her to work in that country.

The friend, who was attracted to Beatrice, offered to welcome her in his home at any time. As for the job, he would inquire with his acquaintances and then inform her..

After three weeks the response came from the United States: if Beatrice wanted the job she would have to go personally for an interview with a company that was looking for bilingual Italian-English staff. She had two weeks' time to do that.

Beatrice had just completed the documents necessary for expatriation when Angelo had the flight accident.

She had just time to pay him a short visit at

the hospital before leaving.

She never spoke to anyone about what had happened between her and Angelo.

She did not want to spoil the relationship that was being re-established between the man and her sister, who was assisting him in the hospital.

Angelo would forget her and she would forget him.

Once she began working in the United States, her choice was consolidated, so much so that she decided not to even attend her sister's wedding.

Alice, for her part, kept thinking that something had happened between them.

But she didn't really want to find out.

So Alice and Beatrice did not see each other again for a very long time, although they did not fail to occasionally exchange news about their lives.

The most beautiful piece of news was when Bea informed Alice that she (Alice) had become the aunt of a nephew named Alex.

It was Angelo, two months after the wedding, who proposed to Alice that she return to live in her country town again, so she could return to work at the Bassano Hospital.

They went to live in a rented apartment, not a very large one but with the advantage of being on the ground floor and with a garden facing the mountain.

Angelo, for his own part, could drive to see his old flying friends, while Alice had acquired lots of practical experience in the field of post-trauma rehabilitation, which the doctors of Bassano appreciated and took advantage.

Alice daydreamed of having children.

Angelo would take care of them, she had a good job and could look serenely both towards the future and towards the clouds: now it seemed to her she was able to caress them, she had made peace with them in her heart.

Everything went perfectly, but one evening Alice, returning from work, felt the ground give in under her feet when her husband told her that he thought he was able to fly again.

On that same day, he had driven up to the runway.

It had been a wonderful day, with the

thermal currents making paragliders and hang gliders go up alongside the mountain like corks shot from a bottle of sparkling wine.

On the runway a disabled man in the wheelchair, helped by his friends, was tying himself to a harness designed specifically for his particular needs.

When the wind was propitious, the wheelchair began to run downhill and take off.

As he looked on, Angelo sniffed the air and once again felt like a bird of prey.

He sensed the wind whirling around him and calling him to take flight. "If that man can do it while he's in a wheelchair, I, who can walk, can do it too," he thought enthusiastically.

He would have two small wheels applied under the frame of a hang glider so he could take off without anyone's help.

Then he would use the same wheels in landing, a bit like planes do.

As Angelo was telling her about that, Alice at first believed he was joking, but then she realized that he meant it. She got very angry and swore to him that if he carried out his plans she would leave him forever.

The woman left the house slamming the door, but Angelo didn't change his mind.

He was convinced that sooner or later she would return, he felt sure of her love, he had already had proof of it.

105

That stubborn man wanted to fly more than he wanted anything else.

He felt happy only when he was in the sky, lost in the blue, above everything and everyone.

It was his way of caressing the clouds.

Angelo pursued his intent and had a hang glider built, modified to make up for his now stable physical defects.

In hang gliding, the pilot normally remains suspended by means of a harness hanging from the structure of the delta, and in the meantime directs it by maneuvering the bar with his hands.

To take off, Angelo had to run down a sloping platform, while supporting with his arms the weight of the aluminum pipe structure.

What with the structure and the canopy, the weight was considerably greater than in a paraglider with only one sail.

It was by no means an easy feat for a person in optimal physical condition, let alone for Angelo with the limitations that made him hardly more fit than a cripple.

However, Angelo eventually made it and resumed his trips among the clouds, while Alice went back to live in her mother's house.

They belonged to two irreconcilable worlds, she to the earth and he to the sky.

Two lives that seemed to touch each other only along the horizon, but never joined.

Living that dimension forbidden by nature to humans, the more dangerous, vertical one, was indispensable for Angelo.

A story that has been repeating itself for who knows how long, in which women try to change men, and men are seldom able to change.

Alice, for the moment at least, refused to take the risks that those challenges entailed. Perhaps one day she would go back to Angelo, accepting the risks he faced.

Or maybe Angelo would get tired of taking those risks and become wiser.

That woman, who had once thanked heaven for bringing her an angel as a partner, now prayed to be able to leave him.

Time stood still for Alice, and she too felt like she was hibernating and waiting to wake up from a bad dream.

She was busy most of the time in the hospital and at home, taking care of her elderly mother.

To bed early in the evening and to work early in the morning – this was her routine.

Her sister Bea was now living permanently in the United States and the scarce news she sent consisted of Christmas and Easter wishes plus a few photos of Alex, who was growing.

But one sad day Beatrice phoned Alice to tell her that Alex was dead. In a sobbing voice, she promised that after the funeral she would take a trip back to Italy to see her sister and mother again.

Alice looked forward to seeing her sister back home, as she too wanted to reconnect that thread that had been broken so many years before.

The long-awaited day finally arrived and Alice went to the Venice airport to welcome Bea.

When their eyes met they smiled, and when they embraced it was a moment of emotion and tears.

As the crying and sobbing subsided, Bea

showed Alice a recent photograph of her son.

She also told her that she had given him that name, Alex because it reminded her of Alice.

Alice looked at the boy smiling at her from the photo and felt her heart almost stop.

She had seen in that smile something particular, already known, familiar.

She went back in her mind to what had happened to them when they were children, to their interminable disputes.

One was happy with a toy even if it was broken, whereas the other was not interested in it if it was not intact and perfect.

And that's exactly how it ended up, that the doll was pulled by the arms until it was torn in two.

But Angelo was not a doll and he could not divide himself between the two of them.

Perhaps one day the two sisters will tell each other their innermost secrets.

Perhaps Beatrice will ask what has happened to Angelo, if he is continuing to fly over their house or if he has disappeared.

Maybe she'll tell Alice all about her affair with him.

Maybe the answer is in the sky.

That sky that had brought a man and a child to two women.

To two sisters.

That same sky that gives men rain and then takes it back.

Index

113

Afterword

This story is based on real facts:
I personally met the hang-glider pilot many years ago, and the nurse who first took care of him in the hospital in Bassano, when he crashed for the first time, then became his wife.

After the birth of their son that stubborn man wanted to fly again despite the physical deficiencies caused by the accident.

Unfortunately, it was a fatal choice which caused his death when he fell with the hang glider that had been modified to enable him to continue to pursue his dreams.

It may seem incredible, but while I was writing this story another person who, on the penultimate Sunday of March 2019 had been on a trip to Venice with me, the following Sunday crashed with a friend's small tourist plane, losing his life too.

I have checked the statistics of paragliding accidents on the internet: they actually have the highest chances of happening compared with other extreme activities or sports. Yet a new even more dangerous sport has begun to be practiced for some time now - I'm talking about wingsuit BASE jumping.

While, in a now distant past, only a few daredevils hovered in the air, opening up new possibilities for humanity, today it seems that the skies are swarming with people who are not afraid of losing their most precious possession.

Whereas in the past heroes risked their lives for ideals of justice and freedom, today there are many people who endanger it as a pastime or for a dream that someone sells to them at a good market price.

I cannot judge anyone's choices, but I still wonder if it is right to incur excessive risks for fun, without taking into account the suffering that one's death can bring to one's loved ones. They are the ones who remain.

Acknowledgements

I thank Arianna Franzan and Luca Valente, who supported
and encouraged me in writing this story.
  I am grateful to my friends of the Romano d'Ezzelino
reading group and A&B for the English translation.

  Finally, my biggest and most heartfelt thanks are for my
wife Bruna for supporting my aspirations, and my son
Matteo, author of the poem quoted in the text.

Date : May /22 /2022